FAITH · VIRTUE

ST. JOHN'S SCHOOL

Given By
Braley Millin

In Honor Of
Alexander

Gertrude, The Bulldog Detective

BY EILEEN CHRISTELOW

CLARION BOOKS • NEW YORK

For Jim

Clarion Books
a Houghton Mifflin Company imprint
215 Park Avenue South, New York, NY 10003
Text and Illustrations copyright © 1992 by Eileen Christelow

Library of Congress Cataloging-in-Publication Data
Christelow, Eileen.
Gertrude, the bulldog detective / Eileen Christelow.
p. cm.
Summary: Gertrude Bulldog stumbles on a real case after her
neighbors plant fake clues to get her to snoop somewhere else.
ISBN 0-395-58701-8
[1. Mystery and detective stories. 2. Dogs—Fiction.] I. Title.
PZ7.C4523Ge   1992
[E]—dc20   91-16376   CIP   AC

W O Z 10 9 8 7 6 5 4 3 2 1

The full-color art was created with gouache
and watercolor crayons.
The text type is 14 pt. ITC Century Book.

As far as Gertrude was concerned, there was
nothing so thrilling as a good mystery story. She often
read three or four before going to sleep at night.

In fact, she liked mysteries so much, she decided to become a detective.

"But this is a quiet town," said her neighbors, Roger and Mabel. "You won't find any mysteries around here."

"Don't be so sure," said Gertrude.

For the next few days, Gertrude practiced her detective skills.

First, she examined the pawprints on Mabel and Roger's front door.

"Why don't you examine your own door?" grumbled Mabel.

The next day, Gertrude tried out a disguise, and she practiced following her friends without being noticed.

She even eavesdropped on their conversations.
"Gertrude, I wish you'd stop snooping around,"
complained Roger. "You are driving us nuts!"
"But good detectives always snoop," said Gertrude.

That evening, Gertrude tried out her new super-detective binoculars. They were so sharp, she could see what Roger and Mabel were eating for supper.

"They should be grateful I'm keeping an eye on things," she said to herself.

But Roger and Mabel were not grateful.

"We need to do something about Gertrude," groaned Mabel. "She's always spying on us!"

"I've been thinking," said Roger. "Maybe we could plant a few clues...make her think she's on the trail of some big-time crooks."

"You mean get her to snoop around somewhere else?" said Mabel.

"Exactly," said Roger.

The next day, when Gertrude went out, she found a
sheet of red paper on the sidewalk. She examined it
carefully. It was a note, hand lettered in purple ink.

"Go to Bart's Café," Gertrude read. *"Put this note
on the table. The Gang will contact you."*

"The GANG?" gasped Gertrude. "I wonder who
dropped this!" The only clue was a smudgy purple
pawprint.

Gertrude hurried over to Bart's Café. She placed the note on her table. Soon a waiter handed her another note, written with purple ink on red paper.

"Who is this from?" said Gertrude.

"I never ask questions," said the waiter.

The new note said, "*Watch the museum. It will happen soon. Good luck from the Gang.*"

Gertrude whistled. "I'm on the trail of something big!" she exclaimed.

The museum was only a block away. Gertrude sat on a bench near the front door and pretended to read the newspaper.

Roger and Mabel walked by.

"We're going to the movies," said Mabel.

"I can't talk now," Gertrude whispered. "I'm staking out the museum."

"How exciting!" said Roger.

"Our trick worked," Mabel whispered to Roger. "Now Gertrude should stay out of our hair for a while."

Roger grinned. "She'll probably sit there for days, waiting for something to happen."

But only a few minutes later a scrawny cat, wearing a dark suit, raced up to the front of the museum. He was pushing a baby carriage.

"How odd," thought Gertrude. "Yellow running shoes with a suit."

At the same time, an orange cat hurried out of the museum. She carried something wrapped in a blanket.

"It must be a baby," thought Gertrude.

The orange cat dropped her bundle into the baby
carriage.

"Let's get out of here," she hissed. "Before they find
out it's gone."

"They're kidnappers!" gasped Gertrude.

The two cats pushed the baby carriage down the sidewalk so fast that it was hard for Gertrude to keep them in sight.

"I can't let them get away," she puffed. "That poor baby!"

The cats turned into an alley.

When Gertrude reached the alley, the two cats had disappeared.

"They got away," Gertrude groaned.

She noticed that the alley was muddy.

"I'm in luck!" she whispered. "They left tracks!"

The tracks led Gertrude through the alley to another sidewalk.

"Now which way did they go?" she sighed.
Then she saw two pairs of muddy footprints. They
headed into the Rialto Movie Theater.

Gertrude quickly bought a ticket.

"Call the police," she whispered to the ticket seller.
"Two kidnappers just went into your theater. They
have someone's baby."

"Oh, no!" cried the ticket seller.

Gertrude rushed into the theater lobby. Two cats were coming out of the restrooms.

"They don't look at all like the kidnappers," Gertrude said to herself. "But why do they seem so familiar?"

Gertrude followed the two cats into the theater.
"It's their shoes," thought Gertrude. "Those two are
wearing the same shoes as the kidnappers!"

The cats sat in the front row.

Gertrude sat just behind them.

"We can hide out in here and then make a run for it," she heard one cat whisper. "You still have our bundle, right?"

"Under my coat," said the other cat.

"I was right! It's them!" thought Gertrude. "How can I keep them here until the police come?"

Then Gertrude remembered: She always carried a needle and thread in her bag.

"This will slow them down," she thought.

The cats didn't notice as she stitched their coats to the backs of their seats.

She was making the last stitch when she heard Mabel's voice.

"Gertrude! What are you doing here?"

"Sh-h-h-h!" hissed the audience.

"Sh-h-h-h!" hissed Gertrude. "I can't talk until the police arrive!"

"Police?" cried one cat. "Let's go!"

"I can't," growled the other. "I'm stuck!"

The cats struggled to get out of their seats. Fabric ripped. Buttons popped.

"They are getting away," shouted Gertrude. Then she saw the bundle drop to the floor.

"The baby!" she cried.

"Quiet!" shouted the audience.

"Gertrude! Sit down!" muttered Roger.

Gertrude lunged and grabbed the bundle.

"It's not a baby!" she said.

A policewoman hurried down the aisle. She focused her flashlight on Gertrude.

"It's the ruby urn that was just stolen from the museum!" the policewoman said. "Where did you get it?"

"Those kidnappers took it," said Gertrude.

"Kidnappers?" said the policewoman. "These crooks are art thieves!"

"Really?" gasped Mabel and Roger.

"I should have guessed," said Gertrude.

"We've been looking for them for weeks," said the policewoman. "How did you find them?"

"These notes led me to them," said Gertrude.

"I'd like to examine those," said the policewoman.

"But why?" gasped Roger.

"Pawprints," said the policewoman. "We're still looking for the other members of the gang."

Mabel scowled at Roger. "Guess whose pawprints are on those notes?" she whispered.

After the police took the cats off to jail, Gertrude treated Roger and Mabel to ice cream.

"Don't look so worried!" she said. "The pawprints on your notes were smudged."

"OUR notes!" said Roger. "How did you guess?"

"I'm a good detective," said Gertrude. "I noticed that pad of red paper in your pocket. And Mabel has purple ink on her paw!"